American Vampire

AMERICAN

VAMPIRE

VOLUME TWO

Scott Snyder *Writer*

Rafael Albuquerque Mateus Santolouco *Artists*

Dave McCaig *Colorist*

Steve Wands *Letterer*

Rafael Albuquerque *Cover Artist*

American Vampire created by Scott Snyder

AMERICAN VAMPIRE Volume Two
Published by DC Comics. Cover, text and compilation Copyright ©
2011 Scott Snyder and DC Comics. All Rights Reserved.

Originally published in single magazine form as AMERICAN
VAMPIRE 6-11 Copyright © 2010, 2011 Scott Snyder and DC Comics.
All Rights Reserved. VERTIGO and all characters, their distinctive
likenesses and related elements featured in this publication are trademarks
of DC Comics. The stories, characters and incidents featured in this
publication are entirely fictional. DC Comics does not read or accept
unsolicited submissions of ideas, stories or artwork.

DC Comics, 1700 Broadway, New York, NY 10019
A Warner Bros. Entertainment Company.
Printed in the USA. First Printing.
ISBN: 978-1-4012-3069-2

SUSTAINABLE
FORESTRY
INITIATIVE
Certified Chain of Custody
Promoting Sustainable
Forest Management
www.sfiprogram.org
Fiber used in this product line meets the
sourcing requirements of the SFI program.
www.sfiprogram.org SGS-SFI/COC-US10/81072

Library of Congress Cataloging-in-Publication Data

Snyder, Scott.
    American vampire vol. 2 / writer, Scott Snyder ; pencils, Rafael
Albuquerque.
       p. cm.
    "Originally published in single magazine form as American Vampire
#6-11."
    ISBN 978-1-4012-3069-2 (hardcover)
    1. Grpaphic novels. I. Albuquerque, Rafael, 1981- II. Title.
PN6727.S555A44 2011
741.5'973--dc22
                        2011008934

Devil in the Sand
Part One

Rafael Albuquerque
Artist

Silverton, Colorado, 1936.

THERE A HOTEL IN TOWN?

SURE, THE EL DORADO. RIGHT UP THE STREET.

HNNCCHH

HEY MISTER! YOUR PACK...

YOU GOT A BABY IN THERE? LORD, HE MUST BE FREEZING! LET ME GET HIM SOME WARM MILK.

THAT AIN'T NECESSARY.

WELL AT LEAST GIVE A PEEK--

WAIT!

HSSSSSS

AAAHH!

HSSSSSS

AMERICAN VAMPIRE
DEVIL IN THE SAND PART ONE

WHEN I WAS A BOY, I USED TO HAVE NIGHTMARES ABOUT MONSTERS HIDING IN THE SHADOWS OF MY BEDROOM.

I USED TO WAKE UP SCREAMING AND STILL SEE THEM EVERYWHERE, IN EVERY DARK CORNER.

I WOULDN'T GO BACK TO SLEEP UNTIL MY FATHER LIT THE LAMPS AND PROVED THE CORNERS AND CLOSETS WERE ALL *CLEAR.*

I'M A MAN NOW. I RECENTLY LAID MY FATHER TO REST AND WHEN I CAN'T SLEEP, I GO WALKING.

LOOKING AROUND, I'M STRUCK BY HOW *BRIGHT* THE DAMN NIGHT'S BECOME. IT MAKES ME WONDER...

WHAT HAPPENS TO THOSE CHILDHOOD MONSTERS WHEN THERE ARE NO MORE *SHADOWS* TO HIDE IN? DO THEY LEAVE? DO THEY MOVE ON?

OR DO THEY SIMPLY LEARN HOW TO LIVE IN THE *LIGHT?*

HEY TY. HOW'S YOUR POP?

HANGING IN THERE, THANKS. I'M HEADED OVER TO THE CLINIC TO SEE HIM IN AN HOUR.

THEN YOU'RE JUST COMING OFF THE NIGHT SHIFT.

WHICH MEANS IF ANYONE VISITED MR. BEAULIEU LAST NIGHT...

...YOU WOULD HAVE RODE THEM UP HERE.

I...

IT'S OKAY.

HE HAD A LADY FRIEND VISIT HIM. BUT THAT WAS EARLY, JUST AS I WAS STARTING.

GREAT. SO WHO'S HIS MISTRESS? A SHOWGIRL? PLEASE TELL ME SHE'S NO ONE NOTABLE.

NO, SHE WAS... SHE WAS A VAMP.

A PARTY GIRL. WELL, THAT'S MANAGEABLE, THANK GOD. WHAT STABLE WAS SHE FROM?

THE FRONTIER.

GOD DAMMIT.

MR. STAR, I'M GOING TO NEED TO USE YOUR PHONE.

BY **BOTH** THE MEN IN MY LIFE.

SO HE'S A BOY TODAY?

OH THE VERDICT IS IN. ONLY A BOY COULD BE SO DAMN **ORNERY**...

NOW... WHAT TROUBLE?

BEEN A MURDER, LILLY. IT'S BAD. WE GOT **JIM SMOKE** TO TALK TO...

LILLY? YOU THERE?

LET SOMEONE ELSE DO IT, CASHEL. PLEASE...

YOU CAN'T CONTROL YOURSELF AROUND HIM. LAST TIME YOU QUESTIONED HIM--

THAT WAS DIFFERENT.

I WAS QUESTIONING HIM ABOUT POP'S MURDER, LIL.

YOU'RE ALWAYS GOING TO BE QUESTIONING ABOUT YOUR FATHER'S MURDER, CASH, DON'T YOU SEE THAT?

BUT UNTIL YOU HAVE PROOF, HE'S JUST ANOTHER CITIZEN YOU'RE SWORN TO PROTECT... CASH?

I GOT TO GO, BABY...

I'LL BE HOME SOON.

Devil in the Sand

Part Two

Rafael Albuquerque
Mateus Santolouco
(pages 37-39)
Artists

THAT'S WHAT EVERYONE *THINKS*--THEY THINK BEING A COP IS ABOUT PUNISHING PEOPLE FOR DOING WRONG.

BUT THAT'S NOT TRUE. YOU *KNOW* IT ISN'T. IT'S ABOUT *BELIEVING* IN PEOPLE, BELIEVING IN THE *GOOD*.

IN THE WILL OF PEOPLE TO DO WHAT'S RIGHT DESPITE THEIR OWN INSTINCTS. YOU'RE GOOD AT THAT. BETTER THAN I AM. BETTER THAN I EVER WAS.

TSSS. BULLSHIT.

NO, IT'S TRUE. I'M *LOSING IT*, CASHEL. I TRY TO BE HOPEFUL ABOUT *THIS PLACE*, ABOUT *THESE PEOPLE*... TO BELIEVE WE'LL CLEAN OURSELVES UP WHEN THE DAM'S DONE, BUT I DON'T KNOW ANYMORE.

I LOOK AROUND AND ALL I SEE IS A *NIGHTMARE*.

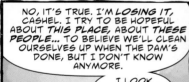

YOU THINK I DON'T FEEL THE SAME?

I'M SURE YOU DO. DIFFERENCE IS, YOU CAN'T HELP SEEING PAST IT. YOU COULDN'T GIVE UP ON THE GOOD IF YOU *WANTED TO*. THAT'S WHAT MAKES YOU--YOU.

IF I WERE YOU THOUGH, FOR THE SAKE OF THAT BABY, I'D *TRY*.

MY FATHER WAS RIGHT--NO MATTER *HOW MUCH* I WANT TO, NO MATTER *HOW MUCH* I TRY... I *HAVEN'T* GIVEN UP ON THIS PLACE, YET.

BUT ON NIGHTS LIKE *THIS*, IT'S HARD TO IMAGINE THAT THIS STRANGE *NEW CITY* OUTSIDE MY WINDOW WASN'T THERE ALL ALONG, *HIDING* INSIDE THE ONE I KNEW...

...WAITING TO BE BORN.

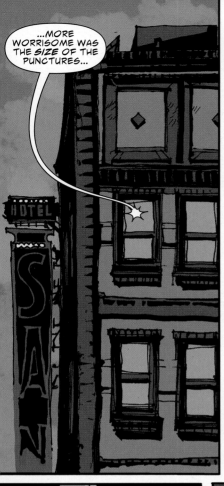

...MORE WORRISOME WAS THE *SIZE* OF THE PUNCTURES...

...THE RADIUS OF THE *FANG*, LIKELY LOCATED AT THE SECOND MAXILLARY INCISOR, CHARTS AT NEARLY NINE MILLIMETERS--TOO BIG FOR A COMMON *CARPATHIAN.*

WHRRRRRRR

MY GUESS IS SOMETHING *OLDER.* PRE-GENOCIDE. MAYBE GAELIC... STOP TAPE.

NOK NOK

WHAT DO YOU THINK?

ABOUT THE TARGET? WELL, ITS FAMILIARITY WITH THE TOWN SUGGESTS THAT IN ITS *HUMAN FORM,* IT RESIDES *HERE.*

SO SOMEONE *LOCAL,* WHO KNOWS THE PLACE AND ITS PEOPLE--WHO TRANSFORMS AND KILLS.

AND CLEARLY WHOEVER IT IS, THEY'RE TRYING TO *DISRUPT* CONSTRUCTION ON THE DAM FOR REASONS THAT--

FELICIA...

I WAS TALKING ABOUT WHAT *HAPPENED* TODAY.

OH...

JACK, I KNOW I MESSED UP, ALMOST BLEW OUR COVER.

AND I KNOW I WASN'T THE COUNCIL'S *FIRST* CHOICE TO JUNIOR YOU ON THIS ONE, WHAT WITH *SWEET* STATIONED HERE, AND MY *PERSONAL* HISTORY WITH HIM.

BUT YOU KNEW I WANTED IT...AND I *OWE* YOU ONE.

APOLOGY ACCEPTED.

JUST TRY TO REMEMBER SOMETHING.... EVERY ONE WHO JOINS THE *VASSALS* HAS A *PERSONAL GRUDGE* TO SETTLE... *NO ONE* JOINS WHO DOESN'T.

AND FOR THE RECORD, I AGREE ON YOUR THEORY. EXCEPT FOR *ONE THING*-- WHOEVER'S DOING THIS ISN'T DOING IT JUST TO SLOW THINGS DOWN ON THAT DAM...

THEY HAVE A SCORE TO SETTLE WITH THE PEOPLE *BUILDING* IT.

BOO.

IT'S NOTHING LESS THAN AN AMERICAN PYRAMID.

THAT'S ALL VERY INTERESTING, *MR. FILMOT*, BUT YOU DIDN'T ANSWER MY QUESTION. IS THERE *ANYONE* YOU'D LIST AS AN *ENEMY* TO MR. BEAULIEU? ANYONE WHO'D WANT TO HARM HIM, YOU, OR THE OTHER MEMBERS OF YOUR *CONSORTIUM OF FOUR*?

YOU'RE NOT LISTENING, CHIEF McCOGAN. THE DAM IS OUR *GIZA*.

AND IF YOU THINK THOSE BENT AND SUN-SCORCHED MEN WHO CONSTRUCTED THE PYRAMIDS DIDN'T SOMETIMES WANT TO *HARM* THEIR BOSSES, OR THE PHARAOHS THEMSELVES...

THEN, YOUNG MAN, YOU DON'T KNOW YOUR *HISTORY*.

SO IF YOU WANT SUSPECTS IN MR. BEAULIEU'S MURDER, CHIEF McCOGAN, I CAN PROVIDE YOU WITH A LIST OF OH, SAY, ABOUT 3,000.

FINE. YOU JUST START AT THE TOP AND WORK DOWN 'TIL I SAY WHEN.

YOU'RE MISSING MY POINT, CHIE--

OH, I GET YOUR POINT JUST FINE. THIS IS A PYRAMID AND YOU, MR. BEAULIEU, AND THE OTHER TWO CONSORTIUM HEADS ARE THE PHARAOHS.

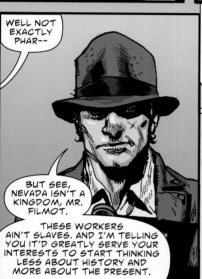

WELL NOT EXACTLY PHAR--

BUT SEE, NEVADA ISN'T A KINGDOM, MR. FILMOT.

THESE WORKERS AIN'T SLAVES. AND I'M TELLING YOU IT'D GREATLY SERVE YOUR INTERESTS TO START THINKING LESS ABOUT HISTORY AND MORE ABOUT THE PRESENT.

BECAUSE YOU'RE ONE OF FOUR MEN RESPONSIBLE FOR BUILDING A DAM. NOW SOMEONE MURDERED ONE OF YOUR THREE CONSORTIUM PARTNERS. LOOK AT THIS PHOTOGRAPH. *DRAINED* HIM OF *EVERY DROP OF BLOOD*. AND WHOEVER DID IT IS *STILL OUT THERE*.

MY GOD, I DIDN'T--

OF... OF COURSE I'LL HELP IN ANY WAY POSSIBLE. EXCUSE ME FOR A MOMENT.

OVER HERE! IT MUST'VE USED THE DRAINAGE DUCT TO GET IN. FELICIA--GET THE LIGHT!

GOT IT!

ALL RIGHT, THAT'S ENOUGH!

LOOKS LIKE IT DROPPED STRAIGHT DOWN.

I'VE HAD MY DOUBTS ABOUT BOTH OF YOU SINCE THE MOMENT YOU SHOWED UP.

JUST CALM DOW--

NOW SOMETHING IS KILLING PEOPLE IN MY TOWN, AND YOU KNOW SOMETHING YOU'RE NOT TELLING ME! WHAT ARE YOU HIDING?! TELL ME NOW OR SO HELP ME-

STOP! PLEASE! I'LL TELL YOU...

FELICIA... DON'T.

TALK.

FIRST, TELL ME THIS, CHIEF McCOGAN...

DEVIL IN THE SAND PART TWO

Devil in the Sand

Part Three

Rafael Albuquerque

Artist

WAIT, I JUST WANTED TO TELL YOU--

TELL ME ABOUT WHAT? THE WEREWOLVES AT THE APACHE? THE GOBLINS AT THE RITZ? DULY NOTED.

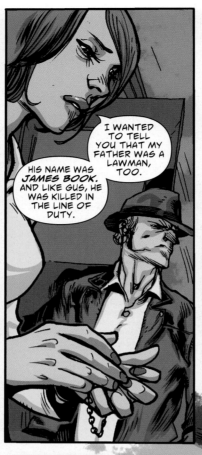

I WANTED TO TELL YOU THAT MY FATHER WAS A LAWMAN, TOO.

HIS NAME WAS *JAMES BOOK*. AND LIKE GUS, HE WAS KILLED IN THE LINE OF DUTY.

MURDERED BY JIM SMOKE. OR *SKINNER SWEET* AS HE WAS KNOWN BACK THEN. SWEET INFECTED HIM WITH HIS BLOOD. MY FATHER DIED FIGHTING THAT INFECTION BEFORE IT COULD TRANSFORM HIM INTO A MONSTER.

SO I PROMISE YOU, DESPITE WHAT YOU MIGHT THINK, THERE'S NOTHING *FAKE* ABOUT ANY OF THIS. IT'S AS REAL AS IT GETS.

YOU DONE?

SURE. I'M DONE. BUT JUST KNOW THAT THERE IS *EVIL* IN THE WORLD. *REAL EVIL*. YOU CAN FIGHT IT, OR YOU CAN HIDE AND PRETEND IT DOESN'T EXIST. BUT EITHER WAY, YOU SHOULD GET READY...

"...DO YOU HAVE ANY WITHOUT WINDOWS?"

OKAY, I'VE HEARD ENOUGH. *GET OUT OF* OUR HOUSE.

EASY THERE, ROMEO.

IF YOU'D JUST LET ME FINISH, MR. PRESTON...

ALL RIGHT, *COOL IT!* ALL OF YOU!

NOW MR. HOBBES... LINDEN.

ASSUMING I EVEN KNOW WHAT MY OWN "WEAKNESS" IS, WHY WOULD I TELL YOU SOMETHING LIKE THAT?

I WON'T PRETEND TO BE ANYTHING BUT YOUR *ENEMY.* I BELIEVE THAT THE BLOOD COURSING THROUGH YOUR VEINS IS INHERENTLY *BLACK* AND *WICKED* AND THAT YOUR KIND ARE AN ABERRATION OF THE *NATURAL ORDER.*

I'VE DEDICATED MY *ENTIRE LIFE* TO AN ORGANIZATION WHOSE *ONLY* GOAL IS THE COMPLETE AND TOTAL ERADICATION OF VAMPIRES--ALL OF YOU, *EVERY* SPECIES.

BUT NOW AND THEN, OUT OF *NECESSITY,* I HAVE STRUCK BARGAINS WITH MEMBERS OF YOUR KIND, IN ORDER TO GET TO MORE PRESSING *THREATS.*

YOU KNOW IT'S FUNNY... AS LONG AS I'VE BEEN THIS WAY, I'VE BEEN WAITING FOR YOU GUYS TO SHOW UP.

WELL NOT YOU SPECIFICALLY, BUT PEOPLE *LIKE* YOU--SOME GANG RUNNING AROUND WITH STAKES AND HAMMERS AND BALLOONS FULL OF HOLY WATER. I MEAN, I KNEW YOU HAD TO BE OUT THERE *SOMEWHERE*.

IT USED TO FRIGHTEN ME, ACTUALLY. I *USED* TO WONDER--WOULD I *SEE* YOU COMING? WOULD I EVEN *FEEL* IT WHEN YOU DID ME IN?

AND I'LL TELL YOU A SECRET. I USED TO WONDER IF IT WOULD EVEN BE A *BAD THING*-- YOU KILLING ME.

BECAUSE YOU'RE RIGHT. ABOUT THE *BLOOD*.

IT DOES HAVE A *DARKNESS* TO IT. I FEEL IT ALL THE TIME, TOO, THAT PULL. AND IT TERRIFIES ME.

THERE ARE DAYS I HAVE TO FIGHT IT OFF. TO REMIND MYSELF OVER AND OVER WHO I AM.

BUT THE FACT IS, I HAVEN'T KILLED ANYONE SINCE 1925. ALL IN ALL, I'VE TRIED TO LIVE A GOOD LIFE WITH THE MAN I LOVE.

AND SO OVER TIME, I GUESS I STOPPED WORRYING ABOUT YOU PEOPLE SHOWING UP.

YOU KNOW THEN.

ABOUT WHAT, *VAMPIRES?*

CHRIST, WHO DO YOU THINK CONVINCED THEM TO *INVEST* HERE IN THE FIRST PLACE?

INVEST?... WHAT THE HELL ARE YOU TALKING ABOUT, INVEST?

IT'S *SIMPLE,* CHIEF McCOGAN. EVEN TOGETHER, OUR FOUR COMPANIES COULDN'T HAVE MADE A PITCH *LOW* ENOUGH TO *OUTBID* THE BIGGER GUYS.

BUT IF SOMEONE ELSE, SOME *SILENT PARTNER,* WERE TO DONATE ENOUGH CAPITAL, SAY SEVEN, MAYBE SEVEN AND A HALF MILLION...

...WELL THEN, OUR GROUP OF FOUR COULD MARCH RIGHT UP TO CAPITOL HILL AND PROPOSE A FIFTY MILLION DOLLAR DAM AT A PRICE OF FORTY MILLION.

A CONSORTIUM OF FOUR COMPANIES, UNDERWRITTEN BY A *SECRET* FIFTH... A BANK--

RUN BY MONSTERS.

Devil in the Sand
Conclusion

Rafael Albuquerque
Mateus Santolouco
(pages 79-81)
Artists

ONE MORE MINUTE?

HANG ON THERE, FATHER.

I'M AFRAID IT'S TIME, SON. SEEMS JUST YOU AND I WILL BE TRAVELING ON--

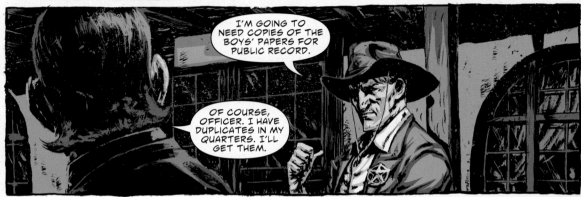

I'M GOING TO NEED COPIES OF THE BOYS' PAPERS FOR PUBLIC RECORD.

OF COURSE, OFFICER. I HAVE DUPLICATES IN MY QUARTERS. I'LL GET THEM.

HOW LONG YOU BEEN ON THAT THING, SON?

ABOUT THREE WEEKS, SIR.

ABOUT?

YES, SIR. I KIND OF LOST TRACK SOMEWHERE IN TEXAS.

I STILL CAN'T BELIEVE IT.

ALL THOSE YEARS... I NEVER SAW HIM KILL ANYONE.

GAELIC-PRIME REQUIRES VERY LITTLE NOURISHMENT. IF YOU KEPT ANY ANIMALS, ANY LIVESTOCK, HE COULD'VE EASILY FED UN-DETECTED.

YOUR FATHER IS PART OF AN ANCIENT SPECIES, CHIEF McCOGAN. *STRIGUS GAELIC-PRIME.* WE THOUGHT IT EXTINCT, ACTUALLY. WIPED OUT BY COMMON VAMPIRES IN THE 1700'S.

BUT THE SUNLIGHT.

CERTAIN OLDER SPECIES LIKE HIS, THE SUN CAUSES THEM PAIN, IT PROHIBITS THEM FROM CHANGING FORM, BUT THEIR SKIN, IT'S TOUGHER THAN CARPATHIA.

AND IF HE TOOK ANYTHING, ANY KIND OF *ZINC TINCTURE...*

HIS INSULIN INJECTIONS...

PLENTY OF VAMPIRES HIDE IN PLAIN SIGHT, CHIEF McCOGAN. ONCE YOU KNOW WHAT TO LOOK FOR, THOUGH...

HOW MANY BRASS, FELICIA?

THIRTY PLUS. MAKING A FEW MORE.

JESUS, I SEE WHY YOU GUYS WANTED TO STOP BACK AT THE HOTEL. WHAT IS THAT, A MINI *FOUNDRY* PRESS?

AS A MATTER OF FACT, YES. METAL GOES IN, *BULLETS* COME OUT.

SHE WAS MY MATE. WOULD'VE BEEN YOUR STEP-MOTHER, I SUPPOSE, IF THINGS HAD BEEN *DIFFERENT.*

WE WERE TOGETHER OVER A HUNDRED YEARS, *BEFORE* THEY CAME FOR US. KILLED OUR CLAN. DROVE US FROM OUR *HOMELAND.*

I'VE KEPT HER BONES WITH ME, HIDDEN IN THE BACK OF THIS PLACE FOR THE LAST FIFTY YEARS.

BUT TONIGHT I'VE BROUGHT THEM OUT. BECAUSE I WANT HER TO SEE... SEE WHAT I'M GOING TO DO TO THE ANIMALS WHO KILLED HER.

YOU'RE DONE KILLING, GUS.

GOD, I'VE MISSED YOU, CASHEL. I'M TRULY SORRY YOU GOT DRAGGED INTO THIS AT ALL. IT'S MY FIGHT. I FOOLED MYSELF INTO THINKING MAYBE YOU AND LILLY WOULD BE GONE BY NOW.

BUT THAT ISN'T YOU, IS IT? THAT'S NOT WHO YOU ARE.

AND THIS IS WHO *YOU* ARE, GUS? WHO YOU'VE BEEN ALL ALONG? A *MONSTER?* A COLD-BLOODED KILLER?

AND IT'LL BE EVEN MORE TOUCHING WHEN WE BURY YOU ALL TOGETHER, IN THIS *TOMB.* YOU, YOUR BITCH, AND YOUR HUMAN BASTARD.

YOU'VE CAUSED YOUR LITTLE DISRUPTION. NOW IT'S TIME TO DIE.

SEE, BUT I THINK IT'S YOU WHO IS ABOUT TO DIE...

...OLD ENEMY.

WE WIPED OUT YOUR WHOLE PITIFUL BLOODLINE WITH LITTLE TROUBLE. WHAT MAKES YOU THINK THIS FIGHT WILL GO DIFFERENT?

WE'RE STRONGER THAN YOU, FASTER THAN YOU. YOU'RE A RELIC OF A BYGONE ERA.

NOW, NOW, VLAD...

DIE, YOU FILTH!

YOU'RE NOT A MAN, SWEET. MY *FATHER* WAS A MAN BEFORE YOU DESTROYED HIM...

BLAM

HSSS!

...THIS IS FOR HIM.

KLIK

BLAM

EASY... EASY.

WHAT DID YOU HIT HIM WITH?

GOLD. MY LOCKET. I ONLY HAVE ONE MORE BULLET...

COME ON, HE'S FAST--

PLEASE... JUST DON'T HURT THEM.

YOU WIN, OKAY?

AW, YOU FOLDING ALREADY, CHIEF? COME ON, BELLY UP TO THE TABLE.

YOU KNOW, I ACTUALLY FOUND IT VERY MOVING, LISTENING TO YOU AND YOUR *DADDY* TALK BACK THERE IN THAT CAVE. I TRULY DID. I CAN'T STOP THINKING ABOUT IT...

CASH, PLEASE...

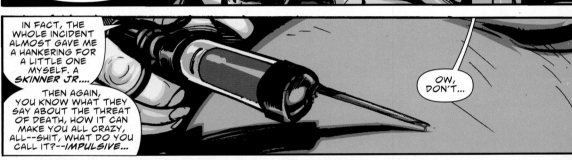

IN FACT, THE WHOLE INCIDENT ALMOST GAVE ME A HANKERING FOR A LITTLE ONE MYSELF. A *SKINNER JR.*...

THEN AGAIN, YOU KNOW WHAT THEY SAY ABOUT THE THREAT OF DEATH, HOW IT CAN MAKE YOU ALL CRAZY, ALL--SHIT, WHAT DO YOU CALL IT?--*IMPULSIVE*...

OW, DON'T...

HONESTLY, I DON'T THINK I'LL BE ABLE TO GAUGE MY TRUE FEELINGS ON THE MATTER UNTIL YOU KINDLY PUT DOWN THAT MAGIC GUN, MISS *BOOK*...

FELICIA. PUT IT DOWN...

I PUT THIS DOWN, HE'LL DO IT...

NOW!

NOW LET THEM GO, *SWEET.*

SEE, *NOW* I CAN THINK CLEARLY!

OF COURSE I DON'T WANT A BABY! I DON'T NEED ONE.

AFTER ALL, GUYS LIKE ME, I THINK WE'VE PRETTY MUCH PROVEN THESE LAST FEW YEARS THAT GOOD OLD-FASHIONED *WILDNESS*-- WELL, IT'S JUST TOO FUN-- AND PROFITABLE--TO LET GO OUT OF STYLE.

AND SO KNOWING I PLAYED A LITTLE PART IN MAKING THIS TOWN WHAT IT IS, AND WHAT IT'LL *ALWAYS* BE... WELL, THAT'S FATHERHOOD ENOUGH FOR ME.

THEN AGAIN, WHY NOT?

OW!

BLAM

CRASH

WE THOUGHT YOU MIGHT SAY THAT. WHICH IS WHY WE SWITCHED GUNS.

CASH, HE'S GETTING AWAY.

GO AFTER HIM.

LILLY, ARE YOU ALL RIGHT?

NO...

"...SOMETHING'S WRONG!"

COME ON... COME ON...

ALL ABOARD!

LAST CALL FOR THE TRAIN TO LOS ANGELES...

WHERE ARE YOU?

THE BULLET...

WHOOOOOOOOOOO

...DAMN.

WHEN I WAS A BOY, I'D HAVE NIGHTMARES ABOUT MONSTERS HIDING IN THE SHADOWS OF MY ROOM...

I USED TO WAKE UP SCREAMING AND STILL SEE THEM EVERYWHERE, IN EVERY DARK CORNER.

AND I WOULDN'T GO BACK TO SLEEP UNTIL MY FATHER LIT THE LAMPS AND PROVED THE NOOKS AND CLOSETS WERE ALL CLEAR.

"SEE SON," HE'D SAY, "NEITHER CREEPIES NOR CRAWLIES."

HER STOMACH, OH GOD...

I'M A MAN NOW, THOUGH... I RECENTLY LAID MY FATHER TO REST.

LILLY...

AND I UNDERSTAND THAT HE WAS LYING TO ME BACK THEN.

BECAUSE THERE ARE MONSTERS OUT THERE. SOME HIDE IN THE CORNERS OF YOUR ROOM. OTHERS IN BROAD DAYLIGHT. HE KNEW IT AS WELL AS ANYBODY.

BUT MY FATHER, RIGHT AFTER HE'D TELL ME THAT LIE ABOUT MONSTERS, HE ALWAYS SAID SOMETHING *ELSE*, TOO.

HE'D BEND DOWN, AND KISS ME ON THE FOREHEAD, AND HE'D SAY, "YOU'RE GOING TO BE JUST FINE."

DINNER and CAFE

AND THAT PART, SEE...

THAT PART I KNOW HE BELIEVED.

I KNOW IT BECAUSE I'M A FATHER MYSELF--YOUR FATHER--AND I BELIEVE IT, TOO. I BELIEVE IT ABOUT YOU, *SON.*

I WILL TRAVEL THIS WHOLE COUNTRY UNTIL I FIND A WAY TO MAKE IT SO.

SNYDER/ALBUQUERQUE

The Way Out
Part One

Mateus Santolouco
Artist

TIME MOVES DIFFERENTLY DOWN HERE IN THE DARK.

WITH NO SUNLIGHT OR SHADOWS. NO WEATHER AT ALL. THERE'S NO FUTURE. NO RIGHT NOW. NOTHING BUT YOUR MEMORIES TO KEEP YOU COMPANY.

BUT THEY KEEP ME SO HUNGRY AND WEAK, I CAN BARELY THINK STRAIGHT. HOW LONG HAVE I BEEN LOCKED UP... WEEKS? MONTHS? I DON'T EVEN KNOW HOW I GOT TO THIS PLACE.

THERE ARE TIMES I DON'T EVEN KNOW WHO I AM ANYMORE...

BUT THEN *HE* COMES HERE. COMES HERE TO HURT ME AGAIN, AND IT ALL COMES FLOODING BACK.

I'M A NEW VAMPIRE, THOUGH--STRONGER AND TOUGHER THAN THE OLD KIND...

MS. HARGROVE. TIME FOR OUR *MONTHLY* APPOINTMENT.

...LIKE HIM. SO THE CHICKEN-SHIT BASTARDS KEEP ME DOWN HERE IN THE DARK... SOMEWHERE.

CHAINED AND STARVING."

AND EVEN SO, HE ONLY COMES BY WHEN I'M AT MY WEAKEST. THE *MOONLESS* NIGHTS. WHEN I *CAN'T* CHANGE.

JUST FIVE SMALL PINCHES TODAY, MS. HARGROVE...

WE'RE MOVING ON TO THE MAJOR SULFATES, SEE? GYPSUM, EPSOM, AND SO ON.

HSSS!

NOW, NOW, AFTER ALL THE TIME WE'VE SPENT TOGETHER.

HOLD STILL. LET'S NOT MAKE THIS HARDER THAN IT HAS TO BE.

AIIIEEEE!

GOTHCA!

OVER AND OVER, HE COMES TO RUN HIS TESTS. SEE IF HE CAN FIGURE OUT WHAT'LL KILL ME.

NOTHING. JUST FOUR MORE TO GO. WE'LL FIND WHAT WE'RE LOOKING FOR SOON ENOUGH...

ALL THE WHILE, I'M TRYING TO FIGURE OUT HOW TO KILL HIM RIGHT BACK.

TIME MOVES DIFFERENTLY UP HERE THAN IT DOES IN THE CITY.

BACK WHEN I LIVED IN LOS ANGELES, I USED TO MEASURE TIME IN THESE TINY PIECES...

...HOW MANY MINUTES I HAD BEFORE I'D BE LATE TO WORK. HOW MANY HOURS LEFT AT THE SERVING COUNTER.

BUT UP HERE, WITH HENRY, TIME PASSES IN THESE BIG CHUNKS BEFORE I EVEN NOTICE.

IT'S LIKE I BLINK AND YEARS HAVE GONE BY.

IT SCARES ME SOMETIMES, BECAUSE UNLIKE ME, HE ONLY HAS SO MUCH OF IT.

AND HERE I AM, ASKING HIM TO SPEND WHAT LITTLE TIME HE HAS LIVING WITH ME, IN HIDING, AWAY FROM PEOPLE, FROM LIFE...

HEY YOU.

IS HE SCARED OF THE SAME THINGS I'M SCARED OF? SCARED OF THE PULL I FEEL INSIDE ME, THE *DARK TUG* ALL THE TIME?

IS HE SCARED OF THE *FUTURE,* LIKE I AM?

SOMETIMES JUST LISTENING TO OUR HEARTS-- IT TERRIFIES ME.

HIS HEART--IT BEATS OUT ALMOST EVERY SECOND OF THE DAY. SO QUICK COMPARED TO *MINE.*

BECAUSE MY HEART IS *DIFFERENT.* IT BEATS ONCE A MINUTE AT MOST. LIKE A LOW, POWERFUL BOOM INSIDE MY CHEST.

HENRY LIKES TO JOKE THAT HIS HEARTBEAT IS THE SECOND-HAND. MINE IS THE HOUR HAND.

BUT THAT'S WHAT FRIGHTENS ME. THAT'S WHAT GIVES ME NIGHTMARES. A FUTURE *WITHOUT* HIM.

THERE ARE TIMES I GET SO SCARED I WANT TO JUST DO IT.

I WANT TO CUT MY FINGER, HOLD IT OVER HIS MOUTH. BUT I COULDN'T DO THAT TO HIM. I COULDN'T TURN HIM INTO WHAT I AM.

MY NAME IS *PEARL PRESTON* AND I'M AN *AMERICAN VAMPIRE.*

TIME MOVES DIFFERENTLY UP HERE ON STAGE.

THERE'S NOTHING BUT THE RIGHT *NOW*, THE MUSIC CARRYING YOU ALONG.

WHOEVER YOU WERE BEFORE YOU STEPPED UP HERE, WHOEVER YOU'RE GOING TO BE WHEN YOU STEP DOWN--IT DOESN'T MATTER.

IT'S WHY I STARTED PLAYING IN THE FIRST PLACE, TO FORGET IT ALL FOR A WHILE, OUTRUN THE *GHOSTS*.

WITH HER, IT FEELS THAT WAY SOMETIMES. I LOOK AT HER AND IT'S LIKE THERE'S NOTHING BUT THE RIGHT NOW, THE RIGHT NOW, THE RIGHT NOW, AND I'M HAPPY.

AIIIEEEE!

YOU WERE GABBING THE OTHER DAY ABOUT YOU'RE FROM *FRANCE,* LAND OF CHAMPAGNE AND ALL THAT.

THAT'S FUNNY, 'CAUSE ME, I'M FROM CHICAGO, LAND OF LOTS OF STUFF.

RED MEAT. BICYCLES. OH, AND ONE THING THEY MADE IN A PLANT RIGHT NEAR MY BUILDING WHEN I WAS GROWING UP...

WAS BOTTLE *CORKS.* FOR SODA POP, BEER, MEDICINE BOTTLES. SEE, CORKS ARE MADE OF CORK *OAK.* FROM CORK OAK *TREES.*

IN OTHER WORDS, WOOD.

PLEASE DON'T...

AW, DON'T WORRY, DOC...

HEAR THAT? YOUR MAN STILL HAS THE *JUICE.*

LOOK AT US, UP LATE WITH THE YOUNG FOLK.

HEY.

THANKS FOR THIS. NOT JUST TONIGHT. *ALL OF IT.*

MMM. WE SHOULD GET OUT MORE OFTEN.

I WAS JUST THINKING THE SAME THING. MAYBE I WILL TAKE ONE OF THOSE CARDS AFTER ALL.

NOTHING. NO GUARDS. NO ARMY. I'M ALMOST DISAPPOINTED.

BUT THEN THE SUN HITS MY FACE, AND I SEE THE OPEN ROAD AHEAD.

FIRST *THING* I NEED TO DO, THOUGH, IS LOOK UP MY *BEST FRIEND*.

BECAUSE IT'S BEEN TOO LONG, PEARLIE.

AND YOU AND ME, WELL, WE GOT A LOT TO DISCUSS, DON'T WE? DON'T WORRY THOUGH. I'M COMING.

I'M COMING, HONEY...

The Way Out

Part Two

Mateus Santolouco

Artist

GET BEHIND ME, HENRY.

WELL, WELL, WHAT DO WE HAVE HERE? A MONGREL BREED OF SOME KIND...

THIS IS GOING TO BE FUN!

SISTER, YOU GOT THAT RIGHT...

H'SSSS SSSS SSSS SSS!

"THERE ISN'T ENOUGH ROAD IN THE *WORLD.*"

I'M SORRY, MISS, BUT IT'S JUST NOT WHAT WE TRADE IN.

MR. ROY, I KNOW AT FIRST GLANCE ITEMS LIKE THESE MIGHT SEEM OUT OF PLACE IN YOUR STORE, BUT YOU DO HAVE *WOMEN* CUSTOMERS, DON'T YOU?

FROM TIME TO TIME, BUT THEY'RE WIVES OF FARMERS AND RANCH-HANDS.

AND BECAUSE THEIR HUSBANDS ARE MEN OF THE LAND, THAT MEANS THESE WOMEN, YOUR *CUSTOMERS,* DON'T THINK ABOUT BEAUTY? BECAUSE I CAN PROMISE YOU, MR. ROY...

ding-ding

...IN THIS HARSHEST OF REGIONS, A WOMAN IS STILL A WOMAN.

DELICATE, VULNERABLE...

...IN NEED OF PROTECTION, ESPECIALLY WHEN IT COMES TO HER... *FACE.*

MY GOD...

CAN I HELP YOU?

DON'T BE SILLY! I'M HERE TO HELP *YOU*! TELL ME YOU HAVE A MINUTE FOR *MARGARET-MARTIN BEAUTY*?

JUST ONE LITTLE MINUTE?

I SUPPOSE... IF IT'S QUICK.

SO QUICK! WOW SWEETIE. YOU'VE GOT A REAL GEM ON YOUR HANDS. I LOVE THE FLOORS. AND THAT SKYLIGHT...

IT'S NOT JUST *YOU* HERE, IS IT?

JUST ME.

SMART. ROOMMATES CAN BE A REAL *PAIN*.

WOULD YOU LIKE A SNACK? I WAS JUST MAKING SANDWICHES.

WHY, SURE...

"...A GIRL'S GOT TO EAT."

UHHH...

CLOSING TIME, CHERRY-ASS MOTHERFUCKER.

KRAK

SORRY, HANK. AIN'T GOING TO BE AN ENCORE FOR YOU TONIGHT.

BEFORE YOU DO IT, I WANT THE NUMBER.

COME AGAIN?

I SAID I WANT THE NUMBER. HOW MANY GUYS LIKE ME DID YOU SELL TO THEM OVER THE YEARS? FIFTY? A HUNDRED?

MORE.

ALL FOR MONEY. BOOTLEGGING HUMAN **BLOOD** FOR THOSE PIECES OF UNDEAD SHIT.

HEY, I'M A SMUGGLER SINCE I WAS 13 YEARS OLD.

THAT'S WHO LITTLE FEET BEALE IS. IN THE TEENS I SMUGGLED GIRLS. IN THE TWENTIES, I SMUGGLED BOOZE. NOW, I SMUGGLE BLOOD. NO **DIFFERENCE** TO ME.

IT MAKES A DIFFERENCE TO **ME**.

GO ON THEN. PRETEND YOU DON'T WANT IT TO HAPPEN THAT WAY FOR YOU.

WHAT ARE YOU TALKING ABOUT?

PRETEND YOU WANT TO DIE A **WRINKLED** OLD MAN IN SOME ARMCHAIR WITH YOUR LADY.

GUYS LIKE YOU AND ME, MEN OF THE ROAD, WE AIN'T FIT TO GET OLD. WE'RE SUPPOSED TO BE OUT IN THE WORLD, ALIVE, PLUGGED IN.

EVERY MUSIC MAN I SOLD TO THEM, EVERY ONE, I'LL BET YOU, HE WENT OUT **HAPPIER** THAN HE WOULD'VE IN THE LONG RUN. EVEN IF HE DIDN'T KNOW IT AT THE TIME.

KEEP TELLING YOURSELF THAT.

"...JUST GET MY OLD BONES HOME."

TAP TAP

ANYONE HOME...?

"WELL HELLO THERE, OLD FRIEND."

I'VE MISSED YOU.

I *AM* LIVING MY LIFE.

DO YOU EVER THINK ABOUT IT? ABOUT... YOU KNOW?

SURE. SURE I DO.

DO YOU?

EVERY DAY. BUT I CAN'T DO IT TO YOU, HENRY. BELIEVE ME, YOU *DON'T* WANT *THIS* IN YOU.

WELL, I FIGURE *WHEN* THE TIME COMES, THAT'LL BE MY DECISION TO MAKE. BUT I WANT YOU TO KNOW, I DON'T EVER WANT TO DO IT OUT OF *FEAR*.

I DON'T WANT YOU TO CHANGE ME BECAUSE WE'RE FRIGHTENED OF THE FUTURE, OR THE PAST OR WHAT'S HIDING BEHIND THIS OR THAT *DOOR*.

NOW, TODAY, THIS IS US. AND I'M *HAPPY* WITH THAT.

YOU'RE TURNING ME INTO A DIRTY OLD MAN.

MY DIRTY OLD MAN.

ME. TOO. COME ON, LET'S GET INTO BED.

WELCOME...

...HOME!

WHO ARE YOU? WHAT ARE YOU DOING IN OUR HOME? HAROLD, CALL THE POLICE.

I'M SO SORRY, MA'AM...

...MY NAME IS *HATTIE HARGROVE* AND I'M JUST IN TOWN TO VISIT A FRIEND... I WANTED TO SURPRISE HER...

HER NAME IS *PEARL?* PEARL JONES?

PEARL, THAT'S RIGHT. I'M AFRAID YOU'RE ABOUT *SIX MONTHS* LATE.

SHE AND HER HUSBAND. WHAT WAS HIS NAME, PERRY? IT STARTED WITH AN "H..."

HENRY.

THAT'S RIGHT, HENRY. THEY *SOLD* US THE HOUSE BACK IN JANUARY. ALL THAT'S LEFT OF THEM IS THAT PHONOGRAPH. SAID THEY DIDN'T WANT IT.

ANY IDEA WHERE THEY WENT?

THEY SAID THEY WERE MOVING TO THE COAST, ISN'T THAT RIGHT?

MERICAN VAMPIRE

SCOTT SNYDER   RAFAEL ALBUQUERQUE

SKIN THE DEVIL

PART 1 OF 4

Unused cover ideas by
Rafael Albuquerque
for American Vampire #6.

Character Designs by Rafael Albuquerque

·CASH·

·SKINNER SWEET·

·ANCIENT VAMPIRE·

COMING SOON
A NEW STORYLINE FOR THE ACCLAIMED SERIES
AMERICAN VAMPIRE
VOLUME THREE

A WORLD WAR II EPIC TALE
OF HEROISM AND HORROR

WRITTEN BY
SCOTT SNYDER

ART BY
RAFAEL ALBUQUERQUE

"THIS IS WHAT WE KNOW..."

"THROUGHOUT HISTORY, *VAMPIRES* HAVE SECRETLY WALKED AMONG US, HUNTING HUMANS AND WIELDING POWER FROM THE SHADOWS."

"BUT AT THE DAWN OF THE 20th CENTURY, A NEW SPECIES OF VAMPIRE WAS BORN IN THE AMERICAN WEST--A NOTORIOUS OUTLAW NAMED *SKINNER SWEET*."

"SWEET EMERGED FROM THE GRAVE A NEW KIND OF VAMPIRE: STRONGER, FASTER AND POWERED BY THE *SUN*. FOR NEARLY FORTY YEARS, SWEET LIVED AS THE ONLY ONE OF HIS KIND..."

"UNTIL 1925, WHEN, FOR REASONS UNKNOWN TO US, HE CREATED A *SECOND* AMERICAN VAMPIRE, HIS ONLY KNOWN PROTÉGÉ--A YOUNG ACTRESS NAMED *PEARL JONES*."

SKINNER S!

"BUT RATHER THAN JOIN SWEET IN HIS SPORADIC WAR WITH THE OLDER VAMPIRE SPECIES, JONES PARTED WAYS WITH HER MAKER, LEAVING HOLLYWOOD WITH HER HUSBAND, A HUMAN MUSICIAN NAMED *HENRY PRESTON*..."

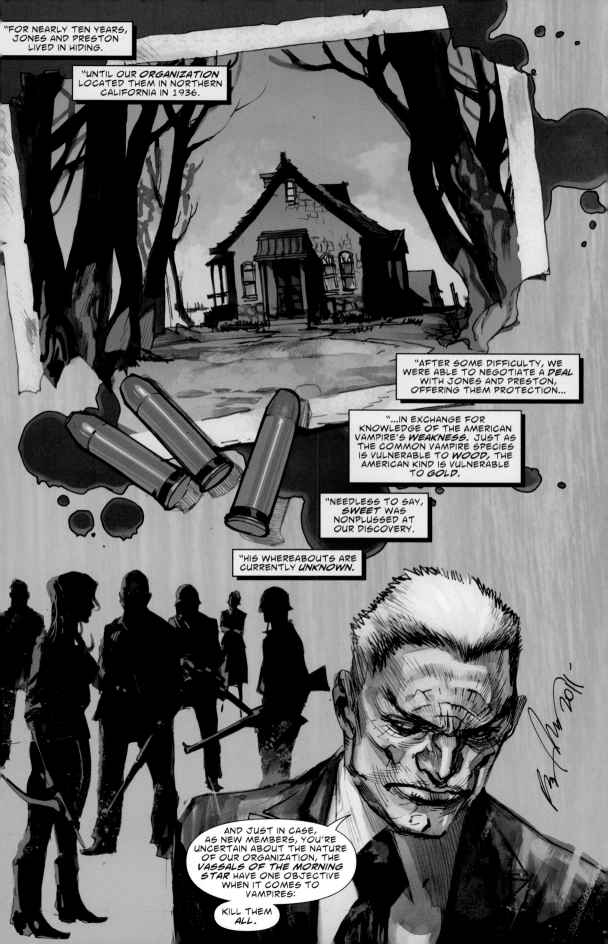

CRACK

SCREEEEEEEEE!

I DON'T HAVE MUCH TIME, PEARL. MY ONLY HOPE IS THAT ~~MY BODY~~...

IS THAT *I'LL* FIND MY WAY BACK TO YOU SOMEDAY.

FIND MY WAY HOME FROM THIS GODFORSAKEN TOMB, AND YOU'LL GET THIS LETTER AND AT LEAST YOU'LL UNDERSTAND HOW THIS ALL HAPPENED.

YOU'LL KNOW WHY I DID WHAT I DID... AND YOU'LL KNOW HOW SORRY I AM, BABY.

SO, SO SORRY.

To be Continued in
AMERICAN VAMPIRE
Volume Three
Coming Soon!

Scott Snyder has written comics for both Marvel and DC, and is the author of the story collection *Voodoo Heart* (The Dial Press). He teaches writing at Sarah Lawrence College, NYU and Columbia University. He lives on Long Island with his wife, Jeanie, and his son, Jack. He is a dedicated and un-ironic fan of Elvis Presley.

Rafael Albuquerque was born in Porto Alegre, south of Brazil, Rafael Albuquerque has been working in the American comic book industry since 2005. Best known from his work on the *Savage Brothers*, BLUE BEETLE and SUPERMAN/BATMAN, he has also published the creator-owned graphic novels *Crimeland* (2007) and *Mondo Urbano*, recently published in 2010.

Mateus Santolouco was born in the city of Porto Alegre, Brazil. He has worked on comics for Boom! Studios, Image Comics, Oni Press and Marvel Comics.